THE GOLDEN BELL

Tamar Sachs

illustrated by **Yossi Abolafia**

translation by **Nancy Wellins**

KAR-BEN
PUBLISHING

KAR-BEN PUBLISHING, INC.
A division of Lerner Publishing Group, Inc.
241 First Avenue North
Minneapolis, MN 55401 USA
1-800-4-KARBEN
Website address:
www.karben.com

Main body text set in Billy Infant Regular 15/22.5.
Typeface provided by SparkyType.

Library of Congress Cataloging-in-Publication Data

Names: Sachs, Tamar, author. | Abolafia, Yossi, illustrator.
Title: The golden bell / by Tamar Sachs ; illustrated by Yossi Abolafia.
Description: Minneapolis : Kar-Ben Publishing, [2019] | Series: Jewish values | Series: Israel | Summary: Itamar, a tailor's son, loses a tiny bell from the hem of the High Priest's ceremonial robe and many years later, an archaeologist finds something gleaming in an ancient drainage ditch.
Identifiers: LCCN 2018007492 (print) | LCCN 2018014501 (ebook) | ISBN 9781541526143 (eb pdf) | ISBN 9781541526129 (lb : alk. paper) | ISBN 9781541526150 (pb : alk. paper)
Subjects: | CYAC: Lost and found possessions—Fiction. | Bells—Fiction. | Jews—Jerusalem—Fiction. | Jerusalem—History—Fiction.
Classification: LCC PZ7.1.S197 (ebook) | LCC PZ7.1.S197 Gol 2019 (print) | DDC [E]—dc23

LC record available at https://lccn.loc.gov/2018007492

Manufactured in the United States of America
1-44594-35506-5/17/2018

A BABBLE OF VOICES WAFTED THROUGH THE SPRING MOUNTAIN AIR OF JERUSALEM.

"I lost a bracelet!"

"It's mine!"

"I found a purse!"

From every direction Itamar heard their cries.
"I found it!" "I lost it!" "Go ahead, take it!"

Someone shouted, "I found a donkey!" And Itamar spotted a delightful donkey, with one black ear and a white tail, being led toward the great stone. The boulder was special. Anyone who had found something would climb up to where the boulder stood, announce his find, and then return the item to whoever claimed it.

They called the boulder the Claiming Stone.

But it wasn't enough just to claim an item. The owner also had to offer some proof that the item was his. Itamar knew that whoever owned the donkey would know it had one black ear and a white tail.

The donkey's brays blended with the cries of voices all around. Itamar would have laughed at the sound—if he hadn't been so worried.

"Are you the tailor's son?" asked a young woman.

"I am," Itamar replied. He was very proud of his tailor father, who was known to everyone in Jerusalem.

"What did you lose?" the woman asked, noticing his worried expression.

"I lost a bell," Itamar said.

"I'm sorry," the woman said, smiling at him. "I haven't found any bells. But I hope you'll find it soon."

Itamar strained his ears and waited to hear someone proclaim, "A bell! Who lost a bell?" Itamar was ready to describe the bell in great detail.

"It's small, it's made of gold and very delicate," Itamar imagined himself saying to the finder. Itamar knew every detail of the beautiful bell. After all, the bell had decorated the hem of a robe that Itamar loved very much.

Itamar often accompanied his tailor father from house to house in the city, collecting items of clothing in need of mending. Sometimes Papa would mend a pair of torn trousers. Other times he might sew up a cloth bag. Once his father was even called upon to mend a hat for a cute baby.

But more than anything, Itamar loved the times when he and Papa would go together to the residence of the High Priest, the most senior priest in the Temple. There they would be given the High Priest's ceremonial robe to mend.

At home, Papa would spread the robe out on his wide wooden worktable.

Itamar would marvel at the beautiful decorations on the robe, the embroidered pomegranates and the little golden bells sewn onto the hem of the garment. Carefully making the little bells jingle with his finger, Itamar would imagine distant realms with each clear ringing note.

This time, however, Papa had asked Itamar to go to the home of the High Priest and collect the robe for mending. The garment was heavy, but Itamar was happy. He hurried home and carefully laid the blue robe on the sewing table. As always, he immediately began to count the little bells sewn onto the hem of the garment. One . . . two . . . what was this? One of the bells was missing!

Itamar was distraught. Again and again he counted the bells, but again and again he got the same result. One of the little golden bells was gone!

Itamar rushed out and began retracing his steps all the way back to the house of the High Priest, searching every street and alley, nook and cranny, for the little bell.

He peered among the rocks, thinking it might have rolled off the path.

He imagined the little
bell tinkling somewhere . . .
all by itself.

Every day since the bell was lost, Itamar had visited the Claiming Stone. During the first few days, he had waited patiently, certain that someone would find the bell. But as the days passed, Itamar began to think the bell would never be found.

Where might the little bell have been lost? he wondered. In what lovely flower bed or under what sun-kissed Jerusalem stone did it now gleam in its golden splendor?

Itamar lost all hope of ever finding it. But the golden bell and its sweet-toned ringing were already planted deep in his heart.

Even when he was all grown up, he still remembered the little golden bell. He loved to tell his children about the blue robe of the High Priest with the little golden bells that were stitched onto its hem, and about one special bell that had been lost and never found.

Many, many years passed. On a spring day in 2011, at an excavation site near the walls of Jerusalem's Old City, a young archaeologist, digging through the ruins, spotted something gleaming in the dirt in an ancient drainage ditch. As she carefully removed the dust and grime from the tiny object with a fine brush, she heard a delicate "ding-ding." Gazing down, the archaeologist recognized that what she was looking at was a small bell.

The Torah, in the Book of Exodus, includes a description of the coat of the High Priest, Aaron:

> "... *pomegranates of blue, and of purple, and of scarlet, round about the skirts thereof; and bells of gold between them round and about.*"

While we can't be sure that the rediscovered bell belonged to a High Priest, we also can't be sure that it didn't....